POSTSCRIPT to

THE NAME

OF THE ROSE

Postscript

Translated from the Italian by William Weaver

UMBERTO ECO

POSTSCRIPT to
THE NAME
OF THE ROSE

A HELEN AND KURT WOLFF BOOK
HARCOURT BRACE JOVANOVICH, PUBLISHERS
SAN DIEGO   NEW YORK   LONDON

Library of Congress Cataloging in Publication Data
Eco, Umberto.
Postcript to The name of the rose.
Translation of: Postille a Il nome della rosa.
I. Eco, Umberto. Nome della rosa. English.
II. Title.
PQ4865.C6P613 1984   853'.914   84-15652
ISBN 0-15-173156-X

Designed by Joy Chu
Printed in the United States of America
First edition
A B C D E

Contents

Illustrations

Rosa que al prado, encarnada,
te ostentas presuntüosa
de grana y carmín bañada:
campa lozana y gustosa;
pero no, que siendo hermosa
tambien serás desdichada.

—Juana Inés de la Cruz[1]

1 "I saw a throne set in the sky and a figure seated on the throne. The face of the Seated One was stern and impassive, the eyes wide and glaring over a terrestrial humankind that had reached the end of its story. . . ." (Adso of Melk in *The Name of the Rose,* p. 41)

Since the publication of *The Name of the Rose* I have received a number of letters from readers who want to know the meaning of the final Latin hexameter and why this hexameter inspired the book's title. I answer that the verse is from *De contemptu mundi* by Bernard of Morlay, a twelfth-century Benedictine, whose poem is a variation on the *ubi sunt* theme (most familiar in Villon's later *Mais où sont les neiges d'antan*). But to the usual topos (the great of yesteryear, the once-famous cities, the lovely princesses: everything disappears into the void), Bernard adds that all these departed things leave (only, or at least) pure names behind them. I remember that Abelard used the example of the sentence *Nulla rosa est* to demonstrate how language can speak of both the nonexistent and the destroyed. And having said this, I leave the reader to arrive at his own conclusions.

A narrator should not supply interpretations of his work; otherwise he would not have written a novel, which is a machine for generating interpretations. But one of the chief obstacles to his maintaining this virtuous principle is the fact that a novel must have a title.

A title, unfortunately, is in itself a key to interpretation. We cannot escape the notions prompted by *The Red and the Black* or *War and Peace*. The titles that show most respect for the reader are those that confine themselves to the name of the hero, such as *David Copperfield* or *Robinson Crusoe;* but even this reference to the eponymous character can represent an undue interference of the author. *Père Goriot* focuses the reader's attention on the figure of the old father, though the novel is also the story of Rastignac; or of Vautrin, alias Collin. Perhaps the best course is to be honestly dishonest, as Dumas was: it is clear that *The Three Musketeers* is, in reality, the tale of the fourth. But such a luxury is rare, and it may be that the author can allow himself to enjoy it only by mistake.

My novel had another, working, title, which was *The Abbey of the Crime.* I rejected it because it concentrates the reader's attention entirely on the mystery story and might wrongly lure and mislead purchasers looking for an action-packed yarn. My dream was to call the book *Adso of Melk*—a totally neutral title, because Adso, after all, was the narrating voice. But in my country, publishers dislike proper names, and even *Fermo and Lucia* [2] was, in its day, recycled in a different form. Otherwise, Italian fiction offers few examples of this kind of title—

Lemmonio Boreo, Rubé, Metello—a handful compared with the legion of Cousin Bettes, Barry Lyndons, Armances, and Tom Joneses that people other literatures.

The idea of calling my book *The Name of the Rose* came to me virtually by chance, and I liked it because the rose is a symbolic figure so rich in meanings that by now it hardly has any meaning left: Dante's mystic rose, and go lovely rose, the Wars of the Roses, rose thou art sick, too many rings around Rosie, a rose by any other name,[3] a rose is a rose is a rose is a rose, the Rosicrucians. The title rightly disoriented the reader, who was unable to choose just one interpretation; and even if he were to catch the possible nominalist readings of the concluding verse, he would come to them only at the end, having previously made God only knows what other choices. A title must muddle the reader's ideas, not regiment them.

Nothing is of greater consolation to the author of a novel than the discovery of readings he had not conceived but which are then prompted by his readers. When I wrote theoretical works, my attitude toward reviewers was judicial: Have they or have they not understood what I meant? With a novel, the situation is completely different. I am not saying that the author may not find a discovered reading perverse; but even if he does, he must remain silent, allow others to challenge it, text in hand. For that matter, the large majority of readings reveal effects of sense that one had not thought of. But what does not having thought of them mean?

A French scholar, Mireille Calle Gruber, has dis-covered subtle paragrams that link the *simple* (in the sense of the poor) with *simples* (in the sense of medicinal herbs); and then finds that I speak of the "tare" of heresy. I could reply that the term "sim-ple," in both uses, recurs in the literature of the period, as does the expression "mala pianta," the tare, or poisonous herb, of heresy. Further, I was well aware of the example of Greimas on the possi-ble double reading (semioticians call it "double isotopy") that occurs when the herbalist is referred to as a "friend of the simple." Did I know that I was playing with paragrams? It is of no importance to reply now: the text is there and produces its own effects of sense.

As I read the reviews of the novel, I felt a thrill of satisfaction when I found a critic (the first were Ginevra Bompiani and Lars Gustaffson) who quoted a remark of William's made at the end of the trial (page 385 in the English-language edition). "What terrifies you most in purity?" Adso asks. And William answers: "Haste." I loved, and still love, these two lines very much. But then a reader pointed out to me that on the same page, Bernard Gui, threatening the cellarer with torture, says: "Justice is not inspired by haste, as the Pseudo Apostles believe, and the justice of God has centu-ries at its disposal." And the reader rightly asked me what connection I had meant to establish between

2 "What were they and what symbolic message did they communicate, those three crisscrossed pairs of lions rampant, like arches . . . ?" (Adso of Melk in *The Name of the Rose,* p. 43)

the haste feared by William and the absence of haste extolled by Bernard. At that point I realized that a disturbing thing had happened. The exchange between Adso and William does not exist in the manuscript. I added this brief dialogue in the galleys, for reasons of concinnity: I needed to insert another scansion before giving Bernard the floor again. And naturally, as I was making William loathe haste (and with great conviction, which is why I then liked the remark very much), I completely forgot that, a little later, Bernard speaks of haste. If you reread Bernard's speech without William's, it becomes simply a stereotyped expression, the sort of thing we would expect from a judge, a commonplace on the order of "All are equal before the law." Alas, when juxtaposed with the haste mentioned by William, the haste mentioned by Bernard literally creates an effect of sense; and the reader is justified in wondering if the two men are saying the same thing, or if the loathing of haste expressed by William is not imperceptibly different from the loathing of haste expressed by Bernard. The text is there, and produces its own effects. Whether I wanted it this way or not, we are now faced with a question, an ambiguous provocation; and I myself feel embarrassment in interpreting this conflict, though I realize a meaning lurks there (perhaps many meanings do).

The author should die once he has finished writing. So as not to trouble the path of the text.

_____

The author must not interpret. But he may tell why and how he wrote his book. So-called texts of poetics are not always useful in understanding the work that inspired them, but they help us understand how to solve the technical problem which is the production of a work.

Poe, in his "Philosophy of Composition," tells how he wrote "The Raven." He does not tell us how we should read it, but what problems he set himself in order to achieve a poetic effect. And I would define the poetic effect as the capacity that a text displays for continuing to generate different readings, without ever being completely consumed.

The writer (or painter or sculptor or composer) always knows what he is doing and how much it costs him. He knows he has to solve a problem. Perhaps the original data are obscure, pulsive, obsessive, no more than a yearning or a memory. But then the problem is solved at the writer's desk as he interrogates the material on which he is working—

3 "Over Christ's head, in an arc divided into twelve panels, and under Christ's feet, in an unbroken procession of figures, the peoples of the world were portrayed, destined to receive the Word. From their dress I could recognize the Hebrews, the Cappadocians, the Arabs, the Indians, the Phrygians, the Byzantines. . . ." (Adso of Melk in *The Name of the Rose,* p. 336)

material that reveals natural laws of its own, but at the same time contains the recollection of the culture with which it is loaded (the echo of intertextuality).

When the author tells us he worked in a raptus of inspiration, he is lying. *Genius is one percent inspiration and ninety-nine percent perspiration.*

Talking about a famous poem of his, I forget which, Lamartine said that it had come to him in a single flash, on a stormy night, in a forest. When he died, the manuscripts were found, with revisions and variants; and the poem proved to be the most "worked out" in all of French literature.

When the writer (or the artist in general) says he has worked without giving any thought to the rules of the process, he simply means he was working without realizing he knew the rules. A child speaks his mother tongue properly, though he could never write out its grammar. But the grammarian is not the only one who knows the rules of the language; they are well known, albeit unconsciously, also to the child. The grammarian is merely the one who knows how and why the child knows the language.

Telling how you wrote something does not mean proving it is "well" written. Poe said that the effect of the work is one thing and the knowledge of the process is another. When Kandinsky and Klee tell us how they paint, neither is saying he is better than the other. When Michelangelo says that sculpture amounts to freeing from the block of stone the figure already defined in it, he is not saying that the Vatican *Pietà* is superior to the Rondanini. Sometimes the most illuminating pages on the artistic process have been written by minor artists, who achieved modest effects but knew how to ponder their own processes: Vasari, Horatio Greenough, Aaron Copland. . . .

NATURALLY, THE MIDDLE AGES

I wrote a novel because I had a yen to do it. I believe this is sufficient reason to set out to tell a story. Man is a storytelling animal by nature. I began writing in March of 1978, prodded by a seminal idea: I felt like poisoning a monk. I believe a novel is always born of an idea like this: the rest is flesh that is added along the way. The idea must have originated even earlier. Afterward, I found a notebook dated 1975 in which I had written down a list of monks in an unspecified monastery. Nothing else. At the beginning I read Orfila's *Traité des poisons*—which I had bought twenty years before at a book stall by the Seine, purely out of loyalty to Huysmans (*Là-bas*). Since none of the poisons satisfied me, I asked a biologist friend to suggest a drug that possessed certain properties (the possibility of being absorbed by the skin when handled). I promptly tore up his letter of reply, in which he said he knew of no poison that would serve my purpose: it was a document that, read in another context, could lead to the gallows.

At first my monks were going to live in a contemporary convent (I had in mind an investigator-monk who read the left-wing newspaper *Il Manifesto*—in Italy even the left has its own heretics). But in any convent or abbey, countless medieval memories survive, so I began rummaging among my files. After all, I was a medievalist in hibernation (I had published a book on medieval aesthetics in 1956, another hundred pages on the subject in 1969, then a few scattered essays, and had returned to the medieval tradition in 1962 for my work on Joyce; in 1972 came a long study of the Apocalypse and the illuminations of the commentary by Beatus of Liébana:[4] so the Middle Ages were kept limber). I dug out a huge amount of material (file cards, photocopies, notebooks), accumulated since 1952 and originally intended for other, still-vague, purposes: a history of monsters, or an analysis of medieval encyclopedias, or a theory of lists. . . . At a certain point I said to myself that, since the Middle Ages were my day-to-day fantasy, I might as well write a novel actually set in that period. As I have said in interviews, I know the present only through the television screen, whereas I have a direct knowledge of the Middle Ages. When we used to light bonfires on the grass in the country, my wife would accuse me of never looking at the sparks that flew up among the trees and glided along the electricity wires. Then when she read the chapter on the fire,

4 "I saw a voluptuous woman, naked and fleshless, gnawed by foul toads, sucked by serpents, coupled with a fat-bellied satyr. . . ." (Adso of Melk in *The Name of the Rose*, p. 44)

she said, "So you *were* looking at the sparks!" And I answered, "No, but I knew how a medieval monk would have seen them."

Ten years ago, in a letter from author to publisher accompanying my commentary on the commentary to the Apocalypse by Beatus of Liébana, I confessed (to Franco Maria Ricci):

However you choose to look at it, I arrived at scholarship by crossing symbolic forests inhabited by unicorns and gryphons, and by comparing the pinnacled and squared construction of cathedrals to the barbs of exegetic malice concealed in the tetragonal formulas of the Summulae, wandering between the "Vico de le Strami"[5] and Cistercian naves, engaging in affable colloquy with the cultivated and sumptuous Cluniac monks, under the surveillance of a plump and rationalistic Aquinas, tempted by Honorius Augustoduniensis, by his fantastic geographies, which explained simultaneously *quare in pueritia coitus non contingat* and how to reach the Lost Island, or how to capture a basilisk when you are armed only with a pocket mirror and unshakable faith in the Bestiary.

This taste and this passion have never abandoned me, even if later, for moral reasons and also material ones (being a medievalist usually implies having considerable wealth and the possibility of roaming among distant libraries, microfilming unheard-of manuscripts), I have pursued other things. And so the Middle Ages have remained, if not my profession, my hobby—and a constant temptation: I see the period everywhere, transparently overlaying my daily concerns, which do not look medieval, though they are.

Stolen holidays under the vaults of Autun, where the Abbé Grivot today writes manuals on the devil, their binding impregnated with sulphur; rustic ecstasies at Moissac and Conques, dazzled by the Elders of the Apocalypse or by the devils thrusting damned souls into boiling cauldrons; and, at the same time, refreshing study of the enlightened monk Bede, rational comforts sought in Occam, to understand the mystery of the Sign where Saussure is still obscure. And so on and on, with unceasing homesickness for the *Peregrinatio Sancti Brandani*, verifications of our thinking carried out through the Book of Kells, Borges revisited in the Celtic *kenningars*, relations between power and masses who have been persuaded checked against the diaries of Bishop Suger. . . .

Actually I decided not only to narrate *about* the Middle Ages. I decided to narrate *in* the Middle Ages, and through the mouth of a chronicler of the period. I was a novice narrator, and in the past I had looked at narrators from the opposite side of the barricade. I was embarrassed at telling a story. I felt like a drama critic who suddenly exposes himself behind the footlights and finds himself watched by those who, until then, have been his accomplices in the seats out front.

Is it possible to say "It was a beautiful morning at the end of November" without feeling like Snoopy? But what if I had Snoopy say it? If, that is, "It was a beautiful morning . . ." were said by someone capable of saying it, because in his day it was still possible, still not shopworn? A mask: that was what I needed.

I set about reading or rereading medieval chroniclers, to acquire their rhythm and their innocence. They would speak for me, and I would be freed from suspicion. Freed from suspicion, but not from the echoes of intertextuality. Thus I rediscovered what writers have always known (and have told us again and again): books always speak of other books, and every story tells a story that has already been told. Homer knew this, and Ariosto knew this, not to mention Rabelais and Cervantes. My story, then, could only begin with the discovered manuscript, and even this would be (naturally) a quotation. So I wrote the introduction immediately, setting my narrative on a fourth level of encasement, inside three other narratives: I am saying what Vallet said that Mabillon said that Adso said. . . .

I was now free of every fear. And at this point I stopped writing for twelve months. I stopped because I discovered something else I already knew (and everyone knew), but that I came to understand more clearly as I worked.

I discovered, namely, that a novel has nothing to do with words in the first instance. Writing a novel is a cosmological matter, like the story told by Genesis (we all have to choose our role models, as Woody Allen puts it).

5 *Templum apertum — Ubi bestia ascendit de abisso:* The beast
of the bottomless pit, and above, the temple with the ark of the
covenant (Rev. 11:7,19).

"The beast is roaming about the abbey . . . the great beast that
comes from the sea . . . the Antichrist. . . .   He is about to come,
the millennium is past; we await him. . . ." (Alinardo of Grottaferrata in *The Name of the Rose,* pp. 157–158)

THE NOVEL AS

COSMOLOGICAL EVENT

―――― ――――

What I mean is that to tell a story you must
first of all construct a world, furnished as much as
possible, down to the slightest details. If I were to
construct a river, I would need two banks; and if
on the left bank I put a fisherman, and if I were to
give this fisherman a wrathful character and a police record, then I could start writing, translating
into words everything that would inevitably hap-
pen. What does a fisherman do? He fishes (and
thence a whole sequence of actions, more or less
obligatory). And then what happens? Either the
fish are biting or they are not. If they bite, the
fisherman catches them and then goes home
happy. End of story. If there are no fish, since he
is a wrathful type he will perhaps become angry.
Perhaps he will break his fishing rod. This is not
much; still, it is already a sketch. But there is an
Indian proverb that goes, "Sit on the bank of a
river and wait: your enemy's corpse will soon float
by." And what if a corpse were to come down the

stream—since this possibility is inherent in an intertextual area like a river? We must also bear in mind that my fisherman has a police record. Will he want to risk trouble? What will he do? Will he run away and pretend not to have seen the corpse? Will he feel vulnerable, because this, after all, is the corpse of the man he hated? Wrathful as he is, will he fly into a rage because he was not able to wreak personally his longed-for vengeance? As you see, as soon as one's invented world has been furnished just a little, there is already the beginning of a story. There is already the beginning of a style, too, because a fisherman who is fishing should establish a slow, fluvial pace, cadenced by his waiting, which should be patient but also marked by the fits of his impatient wrath. The problem is to construct the world: the words will practically come on their own. *Rem tene, verba sequentur:* grasp the subject, and the words will follow. This, I believe, is the opposite of what happens with poetry, which is more a case of *verba tene, res sequentur:* grasp the words, and the subject will follow.

The first year of work on my novel was devoted to the construction of the world. Long registers of all the books that could be found in a medieval library. Lists of names and personal data for many characters, a number of whom were then excluded from the story. In other words, I had to know who the rest of the monks were, those who do not appear in the book. It was not necessary for the reader to know them, but I had to know them. Who ever said that fiction must compete with the city directory? Perhaps it must also compete with the planning board. Therefore I conducted long architectural investigations, studying photographs and floor plans in the encyclopedia of architecture, to establish the arrangement of the abbey, the distances, even the number of steps in a spiral staircase. The film director Marco Ferreri once said to me that my dialogue is like a movie's because it lasts exactly the right length of time. It had to. When two of my characters spoke while walking from the refectory to the cloister, I wrote with the plan before my eyes; and when they reached their destination, they stopped talking.

It is necessary to create constraints, in order to invent freely. In poetry the constraint can be imposed by meter, foot, rhyme, by what has been called the "verse according to the ear" (see Charles Olson, "Projective Verse," *Poetry New York* 3 [1950]). In fiction, the surrounding world provides the constraint. This has nothing to do with realism (even if it explains *also* realism). A completely unreal world can be constructed, in which asses fly and princesses are restored to life by a kiss; but that world, purely possible and unrealistic, must exist according to structures defined at the outset (we have to know whether it is a world where a princess can be restored to life only by the kiss of a prince, or also by that of a witch, and whether the princess's kiss transforms only frogs into princes or also, for example, armadillos).

One element of my world was history, and that is why I read and reread so many medieval chronicles; and as I read them, I realized that the novel had to include things that, in the beginning, had never crossed my mind, such as the debate over poverty and the Inquisition's hostility toward the Fraticelli.

For example: why are the fourteenth-century Fraticelli in my book? If I had to write a medieval story, I ought to have set it in the twelfth or thirteenth century, because I knew them better than the fourteenth. But I needed an investigator, English if possible (intertextual quotation), with a great gift of observation and a special sensitivity in interpreting evidence. These qualities could be found only among the Franciscans, and only after Roger Bacon; furthermore, we find a developed theory of signs only with the Occamites. Or, rather, it also existed before, but either the interpretation of signs then was of a symbolic nature or else it tended to read ideas and notions in signs. It is only between Bacon and Occam that signs are used to acquire knowledge of individuals. So I had to set the story in the fourteenth century—much to my irritation, because I could not move easily in that period. More reading ensued, with the discovery that a fourteenth-century Franciscan, even an Englishman, could not ignore the debate about poverty, especially if he was a friend, follower, or acquaintance of Occam. (I might add that initially the investigator was to have been Occam himself, but I gave up that idea, because I do not find the Venerable Inceptor very attractive as a human being.)

But why does everything take place at the end of November 1327? Because by December, Michael of Cesena is already in Avignon. (This is what I mean by furnishing a world in a historical novel: some elements, like the number of steps, can be determined by the author, but others, like the movements of Michael, depend on the real world, which, in this kind of novel, happens to coincide with the possible world of the story.)

But November is too early. I also needed to have a pig slaughtered. Why? The answer is simple: so that the corpse could be thrust, head down, into a great jar of blood. And why did I need this? Because the second trumpet of the Apocalypse says . . . I could not change the Apocalypse, after all; it was a part of this world. Now, it so happens (I made inquiries) that pigs are not slaughtered until cold weather comes, and November might be too early —unless I situated the abbey in the mountains, so there would already be snow. Otherwise my story might have taken place in the plains, at Pomposa, or at Conques.

The constructed world will then tell us how the story must proceed. Everyone asks me why my Jorge, with his name, suggests Borges, and why

Borges is so wicked. But I cannot say. I wanted a blind man who guarded a library (it seemed a good narrative idea to me), and library plus blind man can only equal Borges, also because debts must be paid. And, further, it was through Spanish commentaries and illumination that the Apocalypse influenced the entire Middle Ages. But when I put Jorge in the library I did not yet know he was the murderer. He acted on his own, so to speak. And it must not be thought that this is an "idealistic" position, as if I were saying that the characters have an autonomous life and the author, in a kind of trance, makes them behave as they themselves direct him. That kind of nonsense belongs in term papers. The fact is that the characters are obliged to act according to the laws of the world in which they live. In other words, the narrator is the prisoner of his own premises.

Another fine story was that of the labyrinth. All the labyrinths I had heard of—and I had Santarcan-geli's excellent study at hand—were outdoor laby-rinths. They could be extremely complicated and full of circumvolutions. But I needed an indoor labyrinth (have you ever seen an open-air library?), and if it was too complicated, with too many pas-sages and inner rooms, not enough air would circu-late, whereas circulation of air was necessary to feed the fire. (This, the fact that the Aedificium had to burn at the end, was very clear to me, but also for cosmological-historical reasons: in the Middle Ages, cathedrals and convents burned like tinder; imagining a medieval story without a fire is like imagining a World War II movie in the Pacific without a fighter plane shot down in flames.) So after I had worked for two or three months constructing a suitable labyrinth, I ended up having to add some slits to make absolutely sure there would be enough air.

I had many problems. I wanted an enclosed place, a concentrative universe; and to enclose it better, it seemed a good idea for me to introduce, besides unity of place, also unity of time (since the unity of action was doubtful). A Benedictine abbey, therefore, its life marked by the canonical hours (*Ulysses* may have been an unconscious model, because of its structure rigidly bound by the hours of the day; but another was *The Magic Mountain,* with its mountainous, sanative situation, where so many conversations could take place).

The conversations posed many problems for me, but I solved these as I wrote. There is a theme that has been scantily discussed in theories of narrative: that of the *turn ancillaries*—the devices, that is, through which the narrator grants the floor to the various characters. Look at the differences among these five exchanges:

1. "How are you?"
   "Not bad. And you?"

2. "How are you?" John said.
   "Not bad. And you?" Peter said.

3. "How," John said, "are you?"
   And Peter replied at once: "Not bad. And
   you?"

4. "How are you?" John inquired anxiously.
   "Not bad. And you?" Peter cackled.

5. John said: "How are you?"
   "Not bad," Peter replied, in a dull voice.
   Then, with an enigmatic smile, he added:
   "And you?"

In all cases except the first two, we see that the author intrudes on the story, imposing his own point of view. He intervenes with a personal comment, to suggest how the words of the two speakers should be interpreted emotionally. But is this intention really absent from the first two, apparently aseptic examples? And is the reader freer in these aseptic cases, where he could undergo an emotional imposition without being aware of it (remember the apparent neutrality of Hemingway dialogue), or is he freer in the other cases, where at least he knows the game the author is playing?

It is a problem of style, an ideological problem, a problem of "poetry," like the choice of an internal rhyme or an assonance, or the introduction of a paragram. A certain coherence must be found. In my case it was perhaps made easier because all the dialogue is reported by Adso, and it is obvious that Adso imposes his own point of view on the whole narrative.

But the dialogue created another problem for me: how medieval could it be? In other words, as I was writing the book, I realized that it was taking on an opera-buffa structure, with long recitatives and elaborate arias. The arias (the description of the great door, for example) imitated the solemn rhetoric of the Middle Ages, and there was no dearth of models for this. But the dialogue? At a certain point I feared it would sound like Agatha Christie, while the arias were Suger or Saint Bernard. I reread medieval romances, works from the age of chivalry, and I realized that, though I was taking just a bit of license, I was still respecting a narrative and poetic usage not unknown to the Middle Ages. But the problem tormented me for a long time and I am not sure I ever resolved these changes of register between aria and recitative.

Another problem: the encasement of the voices, or, rather, of the narrative points of view. I knew that *I* was narrating a story with the words of another person, having declared in the preface that this person's words had been filtered through at least two other narrative points of view, that of Mabillon and that of the Abbé Vallet, even if they had supposedly operated only as philologists (but who believes that?). The problem arose again, however, within Adso's first-person narration. Adso, at the age of eighty, is telling about what he saw at the age of eighteen. Who is speaking, the eighteen-year-old Adso or the eighty-year-old? Both, obviously; and this is deliberate. The trick was to make the old Adso constantly present as he ponders what he remembers having seen and felt as the young Adso. The model (I did not reread the book: distant memories sufficed) was Serenus Zeitblom in *Doctor Faustus*. This enunciative duplicity fascinated and excited me very much. Also because—to return to what I was saying about the mask—in doubling Adso I was once more doubling the series of interstices, of screens, set between me as a biographical personality, me as narrating author, the first-person narrator, and the characters narrated, including the narrative voice. I felt more and more shielded, and the whole experience recalled to me (I mean physically, with the clarity of madeleine dipped in lime-flower tea) certain childish games in which I pretended I was in a submarine under the blankets and from it sent messages to my sister, under the blankets of the next bed, both of us cut off from the outside world and perfectly free to travel like a pair of ragged claws scuttling across the floors of silent seas.

Adso was very important for me. From the outset I wanted to tell the whole story (with its mysteries, its political and theological events, its ambiguities) through the voice of someone who experiences the events, records them all with the photographic fidelity of an adolescent, but does not understand them (and will not understand them fully even as an old man, since he then chooses a flight into the divine nothingness, which was not what his master had taught him)—to make everything understood through the words of one who understands nothing.

Reading the reviews, I realize that this is one of the aspects of the novel that impressed cultivated readers least; or, in any case, I would say that few made a point of it. But I wonder now if this was not one of the features that made the novel readable for unsophisticated readers. They identified with the innocence of the narrator, and felt exonerated even when they did not understand everything. I gave them back their fear and trembling in the face of sex, unknown languages, difficulties of thought, mysteries of political life. . . . These are things I understand now, *après coup;* but perhaps I was then transferring to Adso many of my adolescent fears, certainly in his amorous palpitations (but always with the assurance that I could act through another person; in fact, Adso experiences his love sufferings only through the words with which the doctors of the Church discussed love). Art is an escape from personal emotion, as both Joyce and Eliot had taught me.

The struggle against emotion was hard. I wrote a beautiful prayer, modeled on the Plaint of Nature by Alanus de Insulis, to be said by William in a crucial moment. Then I realized that both of us would be overcome by emotion, I as author and he as character. I as author should not succumb, for reasons of poetics. He as character could not, because he was made of different stuff, and his emotions were all mental, or repressed. So I cut that page. After a friend of mine had read the book, she said to me, "My only objection is that William never has a twinge of pity." I quoted this to another friend, and he said, "That's right, that is the style of his pity." Perhaps this is so. And so be it.

Adso was also useful to me in dealing with another matter. I could have had the story unfold in a Middle Ages where everyone knew what was being talked about, as in a contemporary story, in which, if a character says the Church would not approve his divorce, it is not necessary to explain what the Church is and why it does not approve the divorce. But in a historical novel this cannot be done, because the purpose of the narration is also to make clearer to us contemporaries what happened then and how what happened then matters to us as well.

Hence the risk of what I would call Salgarism.[6] When the characters in Emilio Salgari's adventures escape through the forest, pursued by enemies, and stumble over a baobab root, the narrator suspends the action in order to give us a botany lesson on the baobab. Now this has become topos, charming, like the defects of those we have loved; but it should not be done.

6 "On the table beside the thurible, a brightly colored book was lying open. I approached and saw four strips of different colors on the page: yellow, cinnabar, turquoise, and burnt sienna. A beast was set there, horrible to see, a great dragon with ten heads, dragging after him the stars of the sky and with his tail making them fall to earth. And suddenly I saw the dragon multiply. . . ." (Adso of Melk in *The Name of the Rose*, p. 174)

I rewrote hundreds of pages to avoid this kind of lapse, but I do not recall ever realizing quite how I solved the problem. I became aware of it only two years afterward, when I was trying to figure out why the book was being read by people who surely could not like such "cultivated" books. Adso's narrative style is based on that rhetorical device called preterition or paralepsis, or "passing over." Here is an example from Tudor times: "I doe not say that thou receaved brybes of thy fellowes, I busie myself not in this thing. . . ." The speaker, in other words, claims he will not speak of something that everyone knows perfectly well, and as he is saying this, he speaks of the thing. This is more or less the way Adso mentions people and events as being well known but still does speak of them. As for those people and events that Adso's reader, a German at the end of the century, could not know, since they had taken place in Italy at the beginning of the century, Adso discusses them without hesitation, and in a didactic tone, because this was the style of the medieval chronicler, eager to introduce encyclopedic notions every time something was mentioned. After a friend (not the same one as before) had read the manuscript, she told me she had been struck by the journalistic tone of the story, which was not the tone of a novel but that of a newspaper article. At first I was offended; then I realized what she had unwittingly perceived. This is how the

---

chroniclers of those centuries tell things. And if the Italians still use the word *cronaca* to define the local-news page in the papers, it is because chronicles have gone on being written over the centuries.

But there was another reason for including those long didactic passages. After reading the manuscript, my friends and editors suggested I abbreviate the first hundred pages, which they found very difficult and demanding. Without thinking twice, I refused, because, as I insisted, if somebody wanted to enter the abbey and live there for seven days, he had to accept the abbey's own pace. If he could not, he would never manage to read the whole book. Therefore those first hundred pages are like a penance or an initiation, and if someone does not like them, so much the worse for him. He can stay at the foot of the hill.

Entering a novel is like going on a climb in the mountains: you have to learn the rhythm of respiration, acquire the pace; otherwise you stop right away. The same thing is true of poetry. Just recall how unbearable poems become when they are recited by actors, who, wanting to "interpret," ignore the meter of the verse, make dramatic *enjambements*

as if they were declaiming prose, concern themselves with the content and not with the rhythm.
To read a classical poem in rhyme, you have to
assume the singing rhythm the poet wanted. It is
better to recite Dante as if he had written children's
jingles than pursue only his meanings to the exclu-
sion of everything else.

In narrative, the breathing is derived not from the
sentences but from broader units, from the scansion
of events. Some novels breathe like gazelles, others
like whales or elephants. Harmony lies not in the
length of the breath but in its regularity. And if, at a
certain point (but this should not occur too often),
the breathing breaks off and a chapter (or a sequence)
ends before the breath is completely drawn, this ir-
regularity can play an important role in the economy
of the story; it can mark a turning point, a surprise
development. At least this is what we find in great
writers. A great novel is one in which the author
always knows just when to accelerate, when to apply
the brakes, and how to handle the clutch, within a
basic rhythm that remains constant. In music there is
rubato, but if you rob too much, you end up like
those bad performers who believe that exaggerated
rubato is all you need to play Chopin. I am not talking about how I solved my problems, but about how
I posed them. And if I were to say I posed them
consciously, I would be lying. There is a composi-
tive thought that thinks even in the rhythm of
fingers tapping on the keys of the typewriter.

7   *Ubi mons magnus ardens missus est in mare:* "And the second
angel sounded, and as it were a great mountain burning with fire
was cast into the sea: and the third part of the sea became
blood. . . ." (Rev. 8:8)

"Did the second boy not die in the sea of blood? Watch out
for the third trumpet!" (Alinardo of Grottaferrata in *The Name
of the Rose,* p. 159)

I would like to give an example of how storytelling means thinking with your fingers. Obviously, the lovemaking scene in the kitchen is constructed entirely on the basis of quotations from religious texts, from the Song of Songs to Saint Bernard and Jean de Fécamp, or Saint Hildegard of Bingen. Even readers unfamiliar with the medieval mystics realized this, if they had any ear. But now, if someone asks me the source of the quotations or where one ends and another begins, I cannot answer.

In fact, I had dozens and dozens of file cards with all sorts of texts, and sometimes pages of books, photocopies—countless, far more than I used. But when I wrote the scene, I wrote it all in one sitting (I polished it later, as if to cover it with a uniform finish, so the seams would be less visible). So, as I was writing, I had at my elbow all the texts, flung in no order; and my eye would fall first on this one and then on that, as I copied out a passage, immediately linking it to another. In first draft, I wrote this chapter more quickly than any of the others. I realized afterward that I was trying to follow with my fingers the rhythm of Adso's lovemaking, and therefore I could not pause to select the most cogent quotation. What made the quotation cogent at that point was the pace at which I inserted it. I rejected with my eyes those quotations that would have arrested the rhythm of my fingers. I cannot say that the writing of the action lasted as long as the action (for there are times when lovemaking lasts fairly long), but I tried to shorten as much as possible the difference between the duration of the scene and the duration of the writing. And I say "writing" not in the Barthesian sense, but in the typewriter's sense: I mean writing as a physical, material act, and I am speaking of the rhythms of the body, not of emotions. The emotion, filtered at this point, had all come before, with the decision to liken mystic ecstasy to erotic ecstasy; it had come when I first read and chose the texts to be employed. Afterward, there was no emotion: Adso was making love, not I. I had only to translate *his* emotion into a movement of eyes and fingers, as if I had decided to tell a story of love by playing the drum.

CONSTRUCTING THE

READER

Rhythm, pace, penitence . . . For whom? For me?
No, certainly not. For the reader. While you write,
you are thinking of a reader, as the painter, while
he paints, is thinking of the viewer who will look
at the picture. After making a brush stroke, he takes
two or three steps back and studies the effect: he
looks at the picture, that is, the way the viewer will
admire it, in proper lighting, when it is hanging on
a wall. When a work is finished, a dialogue is estab-
lished between the text and its readers (the author
is excluded). While a work is in progress, the dialogue is double: there is the dialogue between that
text and all other previously written texts (books are
made only from other books and around other
books), and there is the dialogue between the author
and his model reader. I have theorized about this in
other works, such as *The Role of the Reader* and,
before that, in *Opera aperta*; nor was I the inventor
of the idea.

It may be that when he writes the author has a
certain empirical audience in mind; this is how the

founders of the modern novel wrote—Richardson,
Fielding, Defoe—who were writing for merchants
and their wives. But Joyce, too, is writing for an
audience, imagining an ideal reader affected by an
ideal insomnia. In both cases, whether the writer
believes he is writing for a public standing there,
money in hand, just outside the door, or whether he
means to write for a reader still to come, writing
means constructing, through the text, one's own
model reader.

What does it mean, to imagine a reader able to
overcome the penitential obstacle of the first hundred pages? It means, precisely, writing one hundred pages for the purpose of constructing a reader
suitable for what comes afterward.

Is there a writer who writes only for posterity?
No, not even if he says so himself, because, since he
is not Nostradamus, he can conceive of posterity
only on the model of what he knows of his contemporaries. Is there a writer who writes only for a
handful of readers? Yes, if by this you mean that the
model reader he imagines has slight chance of being
made flesh in any number. But even this writer
writes in the hope, not all that secret, that his book
itself will create, and in great quantity, many new
exemplars of this reader, desired and pursued with
such craftsmanlike precision, and postulated, encouraged, by his text.

If there is a difference, it lies between the text
that seeks to produce a new reader and the text
that tries to fulfill the wishes of the readers already

to be found in the street. In the latter case we have the book written, constructed, according to an effective, mass-production formula; the author carries out a kind of market analysis and adapts his work to its results. Even from a distance, it is clear that he is working by a formula; you have only to analyze the various novels he has written and you note that in all of them, after changing names, places, distinguishing features, he has told the same story—the one that the public was already asking of him.

But when a writer plans something new, and conceives a different kind of reader, he wants to be, not a market analyst, cataloguing expressed demands, but, rather, a philosopher, who senses the patterns of the Zeitgeist. He wants to reveal to his public what it *should* want, even if it does not know it. He wants to reveal the reader to himself.

If Manzoni had been thinking of the public's wishes, he would have had the formula handy: the historical novel with a medieval setting, with illustrious characters as in Greek tragedy, kings and princesses (and is this not what he did in *Adelchi?*), great and noble passions, heroic battles, and a celebration of Italian glories from a period when Italy was a land of the strong. Is this not what so many historical novelists, now more or less forgotten, had done in his day, or before him: writers like the artisan d'Azeglio, the fiery and lutulent Guerrazzi, the unreadable Cantù?

But what does Manzoni do instead? He chooses

the seventeenth century, a period of servitude, and lowly characters, and the only swordsman is a scoundrel. Manzoni tells of no battles, and dares weigh his story down with documents and proclamations. . . . And people like him, everyone likes him, learned and ignorant, old and young, devout and anticlerical, because he sensed that the readers of his day had to have *that,* even if they did not know it, even if they did not ask for it, even if they did not believe it was fit for consumption. And how hard he had to work, with hammer and saw and plane, and dictionary, to make his product palatable. To force empirical readers to become the model reader he yearned for.

Manzoni did not write to please the public as it was, but to create a public who could not help liking his novel. And woe to them if they had not liked it. With supreme hypocrisy and serenity he referred to his "twenty-five readers"; it was twenty-five million he wanted.

What model reader did I want as I was writing? An accomplice, to be sure, one who would play my game. I wanted to become completely medieval and live in the Middle Ages as if that were my own period (and vice versa). But at the same time,

8 *Heu locustae ubi angelus perdictionis super eas imperat — Ubi locustae ledunt homines:* And the fifth angel sounded, and out of the bottomless pit came locusts, "and the shapes of the locusts were like unto horses prepared unto battle . . . . And they had tails like unto scorpions, and there were stings in their tails:

and their power was to hurt men five months." (Rev. 9:1–11)

"He told me . . . truly. . . . It had the power of a thousand scorpions. . . ." (Malachi of Hildesheim in *The Name of the Rose*, p. 414)

with all my might, I wanted to create a type of reader who, once the initiation was past, would become my prey—or, rather, the prey of the text—and would think he wanted nothing but what the text was offering him. A text is meant to be an experience of transformation for its reader. You believe you want sex and a criminal plot where the guilty party is discovered at the end, and all with plenty of action, but at the same time you would be ashamed to accept old-fashioned rubbish made up of the living dead, nightmare abbeys, and black penitents. All right, then, I will give you Latin, practically no women, lots of theology, gallons of blood in Grand Guignol style, to make you say, "But all this is false; I refuse to accept it!" And at this point you will have to be mine, and feel the thrill of God's infinite omnipotence, which makes the world's order vain. And then, if you are good, you will realize how I lured you into this trap, because I was really telling you about it at every step, I was carefully warning you that I was dragging you to your damnation; but the fine thing about pacts with the devil is that when you sign them you are well aware of their conditions. Otherwise, why would you be recompensed with hell?

And since I wanted you to feel as pleasurable the one thing that frightens us—namely, the metaphysical shudder—I had only to choose (from among the model plots) the most metaphysical and philosophical: the detective novel.

THE DETECTIVE

METAPHYSIC

———————————

It is no accident that the book starts out as a
mystery (and continues to deceive the ingenuous
reader until the end, so the ingenuous reader may
not even realize that this is a mystery in which very
little is discovered and the detective is defeated). I
believe people like thrillers not because there are
corpses or because there is a final celebratory tri-
umph of order (intellectual, social, legal, and moral)
over the disorder of evil. The fact is that the crime
novel represents a kind of conjecture, pure and simple. But medical diagnosis, scientific research, metaphysical inquiry are also examples of conjecture.
After all, the fundamental question of philosophy
(like that of psychoanalysis) is the same as the question of the detective novel: who is guilty? To know
this (to think you know this), you have to conjecture that all the events have a logic, the logic that the
guilty party has imposed on them. Every story of
investigation and of conjecture tells us something
that we have always been close to knowing (pseudo-

9 "Hunc mundum tipice labyrinthus denotat ille. . . . Intranti largus, redeunti sed nimis artus. The library is a great labyrinth, a sign of the labyrinth of the world. You enter and you do not know whether you will come out. You must not transgress the pillars of Hercules. . . ." (Alinardo of Grottaferrata in *The Name of the Rose*, p. 158)

A drawing of the labyrinth on the floor of the cathedral at Rheims. It is in the shape of an octagon with a smaller octagon at each corner, rather like a corner tower; in these, the builders are represented with the symbols of their craft. The figure in the center is said to be Archbishop Aubri de Humbert, who laid the cornerstone of the cathedral. "The labyrinth was destroyed in the 18th century by Canon Jacquemart because he was annoyed by the children who played there and who sought out the pathways of the maze during the sacred service, evidently for nefarious purposes." (From the jacket of the original Italian edition of *The Name of the Rose*)

Heideggerian reference). At this point it is clear why my basic story (whodunit?) ramifies into so many other stories, all stories of other conjectures, all linked with the structure of conjecture as such.

An abstract model of conjecturality is the labyrinth. But there are three kinds of labyrinth. One is the Greek, the labyrinth of Theseus. This kind does not allow anyone to get lost: you go in, arrive at the center, and then from the center you reach the exit. This is why in the center there is the Minotaur; if he were not there the story would have no zest, it would be a mere stroll. Terror is born, if it is born, from the fact that you do not know where you will arrive or what the Minotaur will do. But if you unravel the classical labyrinth, you find a thread in your hand, the thread of Ariadne. The classical labyrinth is the Ariadne's-thread of itself.

Then there is the mannerist maze: if you unravel it, you find in your hands a kind of tree, a structure with roots, with many blind alleys. There is only one exit, but you can get it wrong. You need an Ariadne's-thread to keep from getting lost. This labyrinth is a model of the trial-and-error process.

And finally there is the net, or, rather, what Deleuze and Guattari call "rhizome." The rhizome is so constructed that every path can be connected with every other one. It has no center, no periphery, no exit, because it is potentially infinite. The space of conjecture is a rhizome space. The labyrinth of my library is still a mannerist labyrinth, but the world in which William realizes he is living already has a rhizome structure: that is, it can be structured but is never structured definitively.

A seventeen-year-old boy told me he understood nothing of the theological arguments, but they acted as extensions of the spatial labyrinth (as if they were the "suspense" music in a Hitchcock film). I believe that something like this happened: even the ingenuous reader sensed that he was dealing with a story of labyrinths, and not only of spatial labyrinths. We could say that, strangely, the most ingenuous readings were the most "structural": the ingenuous reader entered into direct contact, beyond any mediation of content, with the fact that it is impossible for there to be *a* story.

ENJOYMENT

I wanted the reader to enjoy himself, at least as much as I was enjoying myself. This is a very important point, which seems to conflict with the more thoughtful ideas we believe we have about the novel.

The reader was to be diverted, but not di-verted, distracted from problems. *Robinson Crusoe* is meant to divert its own model reader, telling him about the calculations and the daily actions of a sensible *homo oeconomicus* much like himself. But Robinson's *semblable*, after he has enjoyed reading about himself in the novel, should somehow have understood something more, become another person. In amusing himself, somehow, he has learned. The reader should learn something either about the world or about language: this difference distinguishes various narrative poetics, but the point remains the same. The ideal reader of *Finnegans Wake* must, finally, enjoy himself as much as the reader of Erle Stanley Gardner. Exactly as much, but in a different way.

Now, the concept of amusement is historical. There are different means of amusing and of being amused for every season in the history of the novel. Unquestionably, the modern novel has sought to diminish amusement resulting from the plot in order to enhance other kinds of amusement. As a great admirer of Aristotle's *Poetics*, I have always thought that, no matter what, a novel must also—especially—amuse through its plot.

There is no question that if a novel is amusing, it wins the approval of a public. Now, for a certain period, it was thought that this approval was a bad sign: if a novel was popular, this was because it said nothing new and gave the public only what the public was already expecting.

I believe, however, that to say, "If a novel gives the reader what he was expecting, it becomes popular," is different from saying, "If a novel is popular, this is because it gives the reader what he was expecting of it."

The second statement is not always true. It is enough to recall Defoe and Balzac or, more recently, *The Tin Drum* and *One Hundred Years of Solitude.*

It can be said that the "popularity = lack of value" equation was supported by the polemical attitudes of some writers, including me, who formed the Gruppo 63 in Italy. And even before 1963 the successful book was identified with the escape novel, and the escape novel with the plot novel; while experimental works, novels that caused scandal and were rejected by the mass audience, were praised. These things were said, and there was a reason for saying them. These were the statements that most shocked respectable readers, and reporters have never forgotten them—and rightly, because these things were said precisely to achieve such an effect. We were talking about traditional novels with a fundamentally escapist structure, with no interesting innovations with respect to the problems discussed in nineteenth-century novels. And inevitably factions were formed, and good and bad were often lumped together, sometimes for reasons of factional dispute. I remember that the enemies then were Lampedusa, Bassani, and Cassola. Today, personally, I would make subtle distinctions among the three. Lampedusa had written a good, anachronistic novel, and our dispute was with those who hailed it as the opening of a new path for Italian literature, whereas it was, on the contrary, the glorious conclusion of an old path. My opinion of Cassola has remained unchanged. With Bassani, on the other hand, I would now be far more cautious; and if we were back in 1963, I would greet him as a fellow traveler. But the problem I want to discuss is something else.

Nobody remembers what happened in 1965 when the Gruppo met a second time, in Palermo, to discuss the experimental novel (and yet the proceedings are still in print, entitled *Il romanzo sperimen-*

tale, published by Feltrinelli, with the date 1965 on the cover and 1966 in the colophon). Now, in the course of that debate many interesting things emerged. First of all, in his opening paper, Renato Barilli, theoretician of all the experimentalism of the Nouveau Roman, had to come to grips with Robbe-Grillet, with Grass, with Pynchon (it must not be forgotten that though Pynchon is now considered one of the inventors of postmodernism, the term did not exist then—not in Italy, anyway—and John Barth was just getting started in America). Barilli mentioned the rediscovered Roussel, who loved Verne, but he did not mention Borges, because *his* rediscovery was yet to come. And what did Barilli say? That till then the abolition of plots and action had been encouraged, in favor of the pure epiphany in its extreme form of "materialistic ecstasy" (we might say, "I will show you the heavens in a handful of dust," as in the paintings of Pollock or Dubuffet or Fautrier). But now a new phase of narrative was beginning: action was being sanctioned again, even though it was an *autre* action.

I was analyzing the impression we had got the previous evening, watching a curious collage movie by Baruchello and Grifi called *Verifica incerta,* a story composed of fragments of stories, or, rather, of standard situations, topoi, from commercial cinema. And I pointed out that the places where the spectators had reacted with the greatest pleasure were those where, until a few years ago, they would

have reacted with shock and outrage—namely,
where the logical and temporal consequences of traditional action were omitted and the public's expec-
tations might have seemed violently frustrated.
Avant-garde was becoming tradition: what had
been dissonance a few years before was turning into
a balm for the ears (or for the eyes). And from this
observation only one conclusion could be drawn:
unacceptability of the message was no longer the
prime criterion for an experimental fiction (or any
other art), since unacceptability had now been
codified as entertaining. And I remarked that
whereas at the time of the futurists' programs it had
been indispensable for the audience to boo, "sterile,
today, and foolish is the polemic of those who consider an experiment a failure because of the fact that
it is accepted as normal: this means going backward
to the worn-out Utopia of the early avant-garde.
We insist that the unacceptability of the message on
the part of the recipient was a guarantee of value
only in a specific historic moment. . . . I suspect that
we will perhaps have to give up that *arrière-pensée*,
which constantly dominates our discussions,
whereby any external scandal caused by a work can
be considered a guarantee of its worth. The very
dichotomy between order and disorder, between a
work for popular consumption and a work for provocation, though it remains valid, should perhaps be
re-examined from another point of view. In other
words, I believe it will be possible to find elements

of revolution and contestation in works that apparently lend themselves to facile consumption, and it will also be possible to realize, on the contrary, that certain works, which seem provocative and still enrage the public, do not really contest anything. ... Just recently I met someone who, because he had liked a certain product *too much,* had relegated it to a zone of suspicion. . . ." And so on.

Nineteen sixty-five. That was the time when Pop Art was beginning, and the traditional distinctions between experimental, nonfigurative art and mass art, narrative and figurative, were vanishing. This was when Pousseur, referring to the Beatles, said to me, "They are working for us"—not realizing, however, that he was also working for them (and it took the initiative of Cathy Berberian to show us that the Beatles, linked with Purcell, as was only right, could also be performed in recital with Monteverdi and Satie).

Between 1965 and today, two ideas have been definitively clarified: that plot could be found also in the form of quotation of other plots, and that the quotation could be less escapist than the plot quoted. In 1972 I edited the *Almanacco Bompiani*, celebrating "The Return to the Plot," though this return was via an ironic re-examination (not without admiration) of Ponson du Terrail and Eugène Sue, and admiration (with very little irony) of some of the great pages of Dumas. The real problem at stake then was, could there be a novel that was not escapist and, nevertheless, still enjoyable?

This link, and the rediscovery not only of plot but also of enjoyability, was to be realized by the American theorists of postmodernism.

Unfortunately, "postmodern" is a term *bon à tout faire*. I have the impression that it is applied today to anything the user of the term happens to like. Further, there seems to be an attempt to make it increasingly retroactive: first it was apparently applied to certain writers or artists active in the last twenty years, then gradually it reached the beginning of the century, then still further back. And this reverse procedure continues; soon the postmodern category will include Homer.

Actually, I believe that postmodernism is not a trend to be chronologically defined, but, rather, an ideal category—or, better still, a *Kunstwollen*, a way of operating. We could say that every period has its own postmodernism, just as every period would have its own mannerism (and, in fact, I wonder if postmodernism is not the modern name for mannerism as metahistorical category). I believe that in every period there are moments of crisis like those described by Nietzsche in his *Thoughts Out of Season*, in which he wrote about the harm done by historical studies. The past conditions us, harries us, blackmails us. The historic avant-garde (but here I would also consider avant-garde a metahistorical category) tries to settle scores with the past. "Down with moonlight"—a futurist slogan—is a platform typical of every avant-garde; you have only to replace "moonlight" with whatever noun is suitable. The avant-garde destroys, defaces the past: *Les Demoiselles d'Avignon* is a typical avant-garde act. Then the avant-garde goes further, destroys the figure, cancels it, arrives at the abstract, the informal, the white canvas, the slashed canvas, the charred canvas. In architecture and the visual arts, it will be the curtain wall, the building as stele, pure

parallelepiped, minimal art; in literature, the destruction of the flow of discourse, the Burroughs-
like collage, silence, the white page; in music, the
passage from atonality to noise to absolute silence
(in this sense, the early Cage is modern).

But the moment comes when the avant-garde
(the modern) can go no further; because it has pro-
duced a metalanguage that speaks of its impossible
texts (conceptual art). The postmodern reply to the
modern consists of recognizing that the past, since
it cannot really be destroyed, because its destruction
leads to silence, must be revisited: but with irony,
not innocently. I think of the postmodern attitude
as that of a man who loves a very cultivated woman
and knows he cannot say to her, "I love you
madly," because he knows that she knows (and that
she knows that he knows) that these words have
already been written by Barbara Cartland. Still,
there is a solution. He can say, "As Barbara Cartland would put it, I love you madly." At this point,
having avoided false innocence, having said clearly
that it is no longer possible to speak innocently, he
will nevertheless have said what he wanted to say to
the woman: that he loves her, but he loves her in an
age of lost innocence. If the woman goes along with
this, she will have received a declaration of love all
the same. Neither of the two speakers will feel inno-
cent, both will have accepted the challenge of the
past, of the already said, which cannot be elimi-
nated; both will consciously and with pleasure play

the game of irony. . . . But both will have succeeded, once again, in speaking of love.

Irony, metalinguistic play, enunciation squared. Thus, with the modern, anyone who does not understand the game can only reject it, but with the postmodern, it is possible not to understand the game and yet to take it seriously. Which is, after all, the quality (the risk) of irony. There is always someone who takes ironic discourse seriously. I think that the collages of Picasso, Juan Gris, and Braque were modern: this is why normal people would not accept them. On the other hand, the collages of Max Ernst, who pasted together bits of nineteenth-century engravings, were postmodern: they can be read as fantastic stories, as the telling of dreams, without any awareness that they amount to a discussion of the nature of engraving, and perhaps even of collage. If "postmodern" means this, it is clear why Sterne and Rabelais were postmodern, why Borges surely is, and why in the same artist the modern moment and the postmodern moment can coexist, or alternate, or follow each other closely. Look at Joyce. The *Portrait* is the story of an attempt at the modern. *Dubliners,* even if it comes before, is more modern than *Portrait. Ulysses* is on the borderline. *Finnegans Wake* is already postmodern, or at least it initiates the postmodern discourse: it demands, in order to be understood, not the negation of the already said, but its ironic rethinking.

On the subject of the postmodern nearly every-

10 "At a merry signal from the abbot, the procession of virgins entered. It was a radiant line of richly dressed females, in whose midst I thought at first I could discern my mother; then I realized my error, because it was certainly the maiden terrible as an army with banners. Except that she wore a crown of white pearls on her head, a double strand, and two cascades of pearls fell on either side of her face. . . ." (Adso's dream in *The Name of the Rose*, p. 428)

thing has been said, from the very beginning (namely, in essays like "The Literature of Exhaustion" by John Barth, which dates from 1967). Not that I am entirely in agreement with the grades that the theoreticians of postmodernism (Barth included) give to writers and artists, establishing who is postmodern and who has not yet made it. But I am interested in the theorem that the trend's theoreticians derive from their premises: "My ideal postmodernist author neither merely repudiates nor merely imitates either his twentieth-century modernist parents or his nineteenth-century premodernist grandparents. He has the first half of our century under his belt, but not on his back. . . . He may not hope to reach and move the devotees of James Michener and Irving Wallace—not to mention the lobotomized mass-media illiterates. But he *should* hope to reach and delight, at least part of the time, beyond the circle of what Mann used to call the Early Christians: professional devotees of high art. . . . The ideal postmodernist novel will somehow rise above the quarrel between realism and irrealism, formalism and "contentism," pure and committed literature, coterie fiction and junk fiction. . . . My own analogy would be with good jazz or classical music: one finds much on successive listenings or close examination of the score that one didn't catch the first time through; but the first time through should be so ravishing—and not just to specialists—that one delights in the replay."

This is what Barth wrote in 1980, resuming the discussion, but this time under the title "The Literature of Replenishment: Postmodernist Fiction."[7] Naturally, the subject can be discussed further, with a greater taste for paradox; and this is what Leslie Fiedler does. In 1980 *Salmagundi* (no. 50–51) published a debate between Fiedler and other American authors. Fiedler, obviously, is out to provoke. He praises *The Last of the Mohicans*, adventure stories, Gothic novels, junk scorned by critics that was nevertheless able to create myths and capture the imagination of more than one generation. He wonders if something like *Uncle Tom's Cabin* will ever appear again, a book that can be read with equal passion in the kitchen, the living room, and the nursery. He includes Shakespeare among those who knew how to amuse, along with *Gone with the Wind*. We all know he is too keen a critic to believe these things. He simply wants to break down the barrier that has been erected between art and enjoyability. He feels that today reaching a vast public and capturing its dreams perhaps means acting as the avant-garde, and he still leaves us free to say that capturing readers' dreams does not necessarily mean encouraging escape: it can also mean haunting them.

For two years I have refused to answer idle questions on the order of "Is your novel an open work or not?" How should I know? That is your business, not mine. Or "With which of your characters do you identify?" For God's sake, with whom does an author identify? With the adverbs, obviously.

Of all idle questions the most idle has been the one raised by those who suggest that writing about the past is a way of eluding the present. "Is that true?" they ask me. It is quite likely, I answer: if Manzoni wrote about the seventeenth century, that means the nineteenth century did not interest him. Shakespeare rewrote medieval subjects and was not concerned with his own time, whereas *Love Story* is firmly committed to its own time, yet *La Chartreuse de Parme* told only of events that had occurred a good twenty-five years earlier. . . . It is no use saying that all the problems of modern Europe took the shape in which we still feel them during the Middle Ages: communal democracy and the banking economy, national monarchies and urban life, new technologies and rebellions of the poor. The Middle Ages are our infancy, to which we must always return, for anamnesis. But there is also the *Excalibur*-style Middle Ages. And so the problem is something else and cannot be skirted. What does writing a historical novel mean? I believe there are three ways of narrating the past. One is *romance*, and the examples range from the Breton cycle to Tolkien, also including the Gothic novel, which is not a novel but a romance. The past as scenery, pretext, fairy-tale construction, to allow the imagination to rove freely. In this sense, a romance does not necessarily have to take place in the past; it must only not take place here and now, and the here and now must not be mentioned, not even as allegory. Much science fiction is pure romance. Romance is the story of an *elsewhere*.

Then comes the swashbuckling novel, the cloak-and-dagger stories, like the work of Dumas. This kind of novel chooses a "real" and recognizable past, and, to make it recognizable, the novelist peoples it with characters already found in the encyclopedia (Richelieu, Mazarin), making them perform actions that the encyclopedia does not record (meeting Milady, consorting with a certain Bonacieux) but which the encyclopedia does not contradict. Naturally, to corroborate the illusion of reality, the historical characters will also do what (as historiography concurs) they actually did (besiege La Rochelle, have intimate relations with Anne of Austria, deal with the Fronde). In this ("real") picture the imaginary characters are introduced, though they display feelings that could also be attributed to characters of other periods. What d'Artagnan does, in recovering the Queen's jewels in London, he could have done as well in the fifteenth century or the eighteenth. It is not necessary to live in the seventeenth century to have the psychology of d'Artagnan.

In the historical novel, on the other hand, it is not necessary for characters recognizable in normal encyclopedias to appear. Take *The Betrothed:* the best-known real character is Cardinal Federigo, who, until Manzoni came along, was a name known only to a few people (the other Borromeo, Saint Charles, was the famous one). But everything that Renzo, Lucia, or Fra Cristoforo does could be done only in Lombardy in the seventeenth century. What the characters do serves to make history, what happened, more comprehensible. Events and characters are made up, yet they tell us things about the Italy of the period that history books have never told us so clearly.

In this sense, certainly, I wanted to write a historical novel, and not because Ubertino or Michael had really existed and had said more or less what they say, but because everything the fictitious characters like William say *ought* to have been said in that period.

I do not know how faithful I remained to this purpose. I do not believe I was neglecting it when I disguised quotations from later authors (such as Wittgenstein), passing them off as quotations from the period. In those instances I knew very well that it was not my medieval men who were being modern; if anything, it was the moderns who were thinking medievally. Rather, I ask myself if at times I did not endow my fictitious characters with a capacity for putting together, from the *disiecta membra* of totally medieval thoughts, some conceptual hircocervuses that, in this form, the Middle Ages would not have recognized as their own. But I believe a historical novel should do this, too: not only identify in the past the causes of what came later, but also trace the process through which those causes began slowly to produce their effects.

If a character of mine, comparing two medieval ideas, produces a third, more modern, idea, he is doing exactly what culture did; and if nobody has ever written what he says, someone, however confusedly, should surely have begun to think it (perhaps without saying it, blocked by countless fears and by shame).

In any case, there is one matter that has amused me greatly: every now and then a critic or a reader writes to say that some character of mine declares things that are too modern, and in every one of these instances, and only in these instances, I was actually quoting fourteenth-century texts.

And there are other pages in which readers appreciated the exquisite medieval quality whereas I felt those pages are illegitimately modern. The fact is that everyone has his own idea, usually corrupt, of the Middle Ages. Only we monks of the period know the truth, but saying it can sometimes lead to the stake.

———————

I found again—two years after having written the novel—a note I made in 1953, when I was still a student at the university.

> Horatio and his friend call the Count of P. to solve the mystery of the ghost. The Count of P., eccentric and phlegmatic gentleman. Opposed to him, a young captain of the Danish guards, with FBI methods. Normal development of the action following the lines of the tragedy. In the last act the Count of P., having gathered the family together, explains the mystery: the murderer is Hamlet. Too late, Hamlet dies.

Years later I discovered that Chesterton had somewhere suggested an idea of the sort. It seems that the Parisian Oulipo group[8] has recently constructed a matrix of all possible murder-story situations and has found that there is still to be written a book in which the murderer is the reader.

11 "You were awaiting the sound of the seventh trumpet, were you not? Now listen to what the voice says: Seal what the seven thunders have said and do not write it, take and devour it, it will make bitter your belly but to your lips it will be sweet as honey. You see? Now I seal that which was not to be said, in the grave I become." (Jorge of Burgos in *The Name of the Rose,* pp. 480–481)

Moral: there exist obsessive ideas, they are never personal; books talk among themselves, and any true detection should prove that we are the guilty party.

Notes

1 Mexican lyric poet (1651–1695). The lines read: "Red rose
growing in the meadow, you vaunt yourself bravely, bathed
in crimson and carmine: a rich and fragrant show. But no:
Being fair, you will be unhappy soon."

2 Original title of the first version of Manzoni's novel *I promessi
sposi* (The Betrothed).

3 It is curious that in America and the United Kingdom, the
Latin verse reminded many reviewers of *Romeo and Juliet*. It
is curious, because it seems to me that the sense of Juliet's
words is exactly the opposite of that of Bernard's. Shakespeare suggests that names do not matter and do not affect the
substance of the thing-in-itself. Bernard might have agreed
with Shakespeare that names are only arbitrary labels, but for
the Benedictine what remains of the real (?) rose (if any) is
precisely this evanescent, powerful, fascinating, magical name.

4 Part of this text has been published in the second issue of the
American edition of the magazine *FMR*.

5 Address of the Faculty of the Arts in medieval Paris, Rue du
Fouarre, as referred to by Dante, *Paradiso*, X, 137 ("Straw
Street" in Sayers-Reynolds translation).

6 Emilio Salgari was a well-known popular Italian author of
the late nineteenth century who wrote innumerable books of
exotic adventures.

7 Both essays are reprinted in *The Literature of Exhaustion* (Northridge, Calif.: Lord John Press, 1982).

8 Ouvroir de Littérature Potentielle, organized by Queneau, Le Lyonnais, Perec, and others to produce literature by mathematical combinatory means.